You Can't Catch Me!

To Sophie

A Red Fox Book

Published by Random House Children's Books
20 Vauxhall Bridge Road, London SW1V 2SA

A division of Random House UK Ltd
London Melbourne Sydney Auckland
Johannesburg and agencies throughout the world
Copyright © John Prater 1984

3 5 7 9 10 8 6 4 2

First published by The Bodley Head Children's Books 1984
Red Fox edition 1995
All rights reserved
The right of John Prater to be identified as the author and
illustrator of this work has been asserted by him in accordance with
the Copyright, Designs and Patents Act, 1988.

Printed in Singapore

RANDOM HOUSE UK Limited Reg. No. 954009

ISBN 0 09 913821 2

You Can't Catch Me!

John Prater

RED FOX

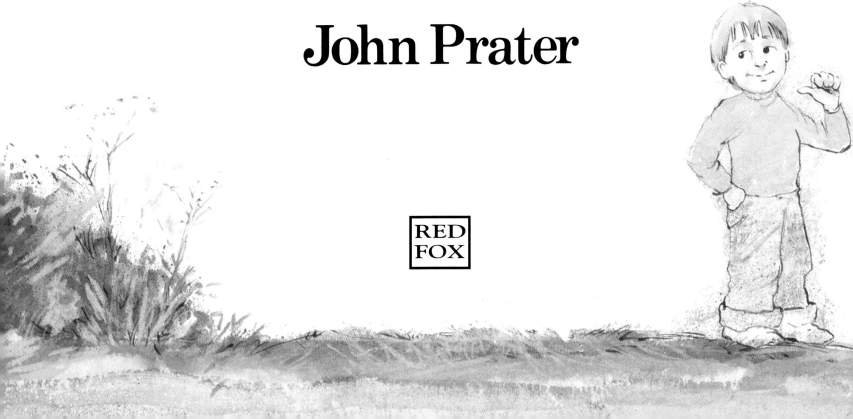

"It's bathtime, Jack," called Dad.
"I hate baths!" said Jack.

"Go and have your bath RIGHT NOW!"
said Mum.
"You can't catch me!" Jack replied.

And he set off down the garden.

"They're coming! I'll hide in here,"
thought Jack.

"He's in the shed!" shouted Mr Crabtree.

Jack slipped nimbly out of the window.

"Mind my vegetables!"
yelled Mr Crabtree as
he joined in the chase.

"You can't catch me!"
said Jack...

and he was right.

Mrs Polly was hanging out her washing.
"Mind my clean clothes!" she shrieked.

"You can't catch me!" said Jack...

and he was right.

"Mind my bike!" shouted Mr Digwood.
"You can't catch me!" said Jack,
as he dashed into the lane.

"Mind where you're going, boy!" warned
Colonel Watt as Jack sped past.

"You can't catch me!" said Jack...
and he was right.

Jack hid in the shadow of a large tree, while the angry grown-ups looked everywhere for him.

"You can't catch me!" he said to himself...

and he was right.

When the coast was clear,
Jack set off again.
"They'll never catch me!"
he thought, but...

Oh! What a mess!

Even worse, Jack couldn't move until
the grown-ups had passed.

"Still, they can't catch me!" he whispered
to his new friend, the pig, and he was right.

No one saw him plod home...

or what he did when he got there.

"Hello!" said Jack. "You
can't catch me!"
But this time, he was wrong.

Some
bestselling Red Fox
picture books